For Rowan, with love from Auntie Mo — MF

For Malaïka and Léo — CS

Text copyright © 2017 by Maureen Fergus
Illustrations copyright © 2017 by Carey Sookocheff
Published in Canada and the USA in 2017 by Groundwood Books

Groundwood Books / House of Anansi Press
groundwoodbooks.com

We acknowledge for their financial support of our publishing program the Canada
Council for the Arts, the Ontario Arts Council and the Government of Canada.

Canada Council for the Arts — Conseil des Arts du Canada

ONTARIO ARTS COUNCIL
CONSEIL DES ARTS DE L'ONTARIO
an Ontario government agency
un organisme du gouvernement de l'Ontario

With the participation of the Government of Canada
Avec la participation du gouvernement du Canada | Canadä

Library and Archives Canada Cataloguing in Publication
Fergus, Maureen, author
Buddy and Earl go to school / Maureen Fergus ; pictures
by Carey Sookocheff.
(Buddy and Earl ; 4)
Issued in print and electronic formats.
ISBN 978-1-55498-927-0 (hardcover). — ISBN 978-1-55498-928-7 (PDF). —
ISBN 978-1-77306-084-2 (FXL). — ISBN 978-1-77306-085-9 (KF8)
I. Sookocheff, Carey, illustrator II. Title.
PS8611.E735B857 2017   jC813'.6   C2016-907997-X
C2016-907998-8

The illustrations were done in Acryl Gouache on watercolor paper
and assembled in Photoshop.
Design by Michael Solomon
Printed and bound in Malaysia

MIX
Paper from
responsible sources
FSC® C012700

BUDDY and EARL
go to school

MAUREEN FERGUS

Pictures by
CAREY SOOKOCHEFF

GROUNDWOOD BOOKS
HOUSE OF ANANSI PRESS
TORONTO   BERKELEY

Buddy and Earl were about to climb a magic beanstalk when Meredith ran into the living room with some thrilling news.

"Today, you are going to school!"

"Hurrah!" cheered Earl. "Getting an education is the first step to achieving my dream of becoming a dentist."

"I do not think hedgehogs can become dentists, Earl," said Buddy.

"With the right education, I can become anything," declared Earl. "And so can you, Buddy."

Buddy was very excited to hear this.

"Can I become a hot-dog vendor?" asked Buddy.
"Yes!" cried Earl.

"Can I become a police officer?" asked Buddy.
"Yes!" cried Earl.

POLICE

"Can I become a fire hydrant?" asked Buddy.
"Absolutely!" cried Earl.

Suddenly, Buddy remembered what he did to fire hydrants.

"I do not think I want to become a fire hydrant, Earl," he said.

"Now is not the time to make hasty career decisions, Buddy," said Earl. "Now is the time to get ready for school!"

"First, we need to eat a nutritious breakfast," said Earl as he began gnawing on Dad's slipper.

"That is not a nutritious breakfast, Earl," said Buddy. "That is Dad's slipper."

"That explains why it tastes so disgusting," said Earl.

"His fancy shoes are tastier," admitted Buddy.

"Next, we need to wash our faces and smooth down our beautiful quills," said Earl.

"I do not have beautiful quills, Earl. Can I smooth down my beautiful ears instead?" asked Buddy.

"Of course!" said Earl.

"Finally, we need to collect our school supplies," said Earl.
"We will need all our toys, your smelly blanket, a big pile of
dirty socks and as much toilet tissue as we can carry."

"Will we also need a snack?" asked Buddy hopefully.

"Absolutely!" said Earl.

Buddy and Earl had just finished gathering their school supplies when Meredith returned.

"You two need to come with me right now," she said. "Otherwise, you're going to be late for school!"

Buddy and Earl did not want to be late for school, so they quickly followed Meredith down the hall to their new classroom.

As soon as Buddy and Earl had taken their seats, Earl said hello to the other students.

None of the other students said hello to Earl.

None of them even looked at him!

"What do you think their problem is, Buddy?" whispered Earl.

"I think their problem is that they are only toys," whispered Buddy.

"That is no excuse for being rude," said Earl irritably.

Earl sat there glaring at the other students until Meredith clapped her hands.

"Good morning, class," she said. "I am your teacher, Miss Meredith."

"Good morning, Miss Meredith," said Buddy politely.

"I'm bored," said Earl. "When is recess?"

"How long until gym? Is it almost snack time?"

Before Miss Meredith could answer Earl's questions, Mom hollered for her to come and clean up her breakfast dishes.

"Children, I'm afraid I must attend a staff meeting," said Miss Meredith. "Earl will be in charge while I'm gone."

After Miss Meredith left, Earl quietly glowed with pride for a while.

Then, in a voice filled with emotion, he said,
"You know, I've always dreamed of being a teacher."
"I thought you had always dreamed of being a
dentist, Earl," said Buddy.
"I prefer to be called Professor," said Earl stiffly.
"Okay, Professor," said Buddy.

Professor Earl led Buddy into the hall.

"Your first class is called Sniffing Things," said Professor Earl.

"I know how to sniff things," marveled Buddy.

"You do?" said Professor Earl in amazement. "Show me!"

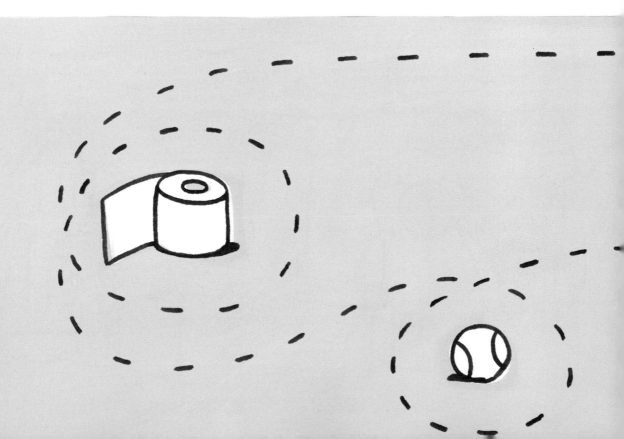

Buddy raced around sniffing
everything there was to sniff.
"Well done," complimented
Professor Earl.

Buddy's next class was Tail Chasing.

"I know how to do that, too," said Buddy eagerly as he began to spin.

"Faster, Buddy, faster!" encouraged Professor Earl.

Buddy chased his tail as fast as he could for as long as he could.

"How did I do, Professor?" he asked woozily when he finally stopped.

"Fantastically well," replied Professor Earl.

"Our final class of the morning is Scratching Itches," said Professor Earl.

"I can scratch itches!" exclaimed Buddy.

Buddy scratched his back, his ears, even his backside!

"Magnificent," declared Professor Earl.

Suddenly, he slapped himself on the forehead.

"Oh, no," gasped Professor Earl. "I almost forgot about the assembly!"

"Oh, no," gasped Buddy. "What assembly?"

"The one where a very special student is going to win a major award!" cried Professor Earl. "We need to get to the auditorium right away!"

Buddy hurriedly followed Professor Earl
to the auditorium.
He helped Professor Earl onto the stage.

"This special student is clever, talented and hardworking," began Professor Earl.

How impressive! thought Buddy.

"He is loyal, brave and kind," continued Professor Earl.

Sounds like a good friend, thought Buddy.

Lifting the major award high in the air, Professor Earl said, "And the name of this very special student is …"

"BUDDY!"

Buddy could hardly believe his beautiful ears.

"Are you sure?" he gasped.

"Yes!" boomed Professor Earl. "So come up here and get your award, Buddy!"

"I am coming, Professor!" roared Buddy. "I am coming!"

Professor Earl gave Buddy his award, a standing ovation *and* a big, prickly hug.

"Thank you, Earl," said Buddy with a happy sigh. "Next to being friends with you, going to school has been the best adventure *ever*."

CLASS DISMISSED